Blue Sea

by **Robert Kalan**

illustrated by
Donald Crews

A Mulberry Paperback Book, New York

10   9

Library of Congress
Cataloging in Publication Data
Kalan, Robert.   Blue sea.
Summary: Several fishes of varying size introduce
space relationships and size differences.
[1. Size and shape — Fiction.   2. Space perception —
Fiction.   3. Fishes — Fiction]
I. Crews, Donald.   II. Title.   PZ7.K123475Bl
[E] 78-18396
ISBN 0-688-11509-8

For Aunt Helen and Uncle Steve
— R.K.
For Hidy and Slank
— D.C.

blue sea

little fish

big fish

swim, little fish

bigger fish

swim, big fish

swim, little fish

biggest fish

swim, bigger fish

swim, big fish

swim, little fish

small hole

there goes bigger fish

there goes big fish

there goes little fish

Ouch!

good-bye, biggest fish

there goes big fish

there goes little fish

smaller hole

Ouch!

good-bye, bigger fish

smallest hole

there goes little fish

Ouch!

good-bye, big fish

little fish

blue sea

Robert Kalan

was born in Los Angeles. He was graduated from Claremont Men's College in 1972. He has taught reading to both gifted and remedial students as well as kindergarten and fourth grade, and completed a master's degree in education at Claremont Graduate School. He is currently living in Seattle, where he teaches a course in writing for children at the University of Washington. His first book was Rain, illustrated by Donald Crews.

Donald Crews

was graduated from Cooper Union for the Advancement of Science and Art in New York City. He has written and illustrated many books for young children, including We Read: A to Z and the more recent Freight Train, published by Greenwillow. He and his wife Ann are free-lance artists and designers, and live in New York with their two daughters.